The Sweetest Victory

by Hillary B. Spangler, MD

Illustrated by Marina Saumell

"Good morning, class!" Mrs. Grizzly said cheerfully. "Open your history books. We are learning about the Great Honey Feud of 1902."

"What is a feud?" Ice, the polar bear, asked.
"Well, it is kind of like a really long argument, but this one was really sticky," Mrs. Grizzly answered.

"Many years ago, the forest had two honey shop owners, Kodiak and Gobi. They were always competing to win all of the honey business in the forest."

"Kodiak and Gobi would do anything to keep each other from selling honey…

They would release each other's honey bees.

They would steal each other's honey pots.

They would even trick each other into being a *Sticky Chicken*."

"What is a *Sticky Chicken*?" Ice asked.

"One bear would hide in a tree and drop honey and feathers from above, making the other look like a really big chicken!"

"They looked so much like chickens, all of the baby chicks in the forest followed them around shouting, *Mama!*" Mrs. Grizzly explained.

"Kodiak and Gobi were tired of being chased by baby chicks, plus they ran out of feathers, so they challenged each other to a honey taste test.

Whoever had the best honey would win all of the honey business in the forest!"

"The next day, the two bears faced each other in the forest square. It was just like an old-fashioned Wild West standoff, but with honey, of course." Mrs. Grizzly said.

"There's only room for one honey shop in this forest, and that's mine!" Kodiak roared.

Kodiak was up first.

"TOO SOUR!" all three judges yelled.

"I think I just swallowed a whole lemon," one judge puckered.

Gobi chuckled and brought his honey to the tasting block.

"Get ready for the best thing you have ever tasted!"

"TOO SWEET!" all three judges yelled.

JUDGE 1
MR. FOX

One judge said, "You would have the perfect honey if you combined your recipes."

"You mean, like work together?" Kodiak asked with confusion.

"Maybe that's not such a bad idea. We would double our honey sales," Gobi said.

"Kodiak and Gobi did the unthinkable, they worked together! They mixed and tasted until they had the perfect recipe."

Kodiak and Gobi brought their new honey back to the judges. "We think you will like this one." The judges ate one spoonful, then another, and then another!

"Delicious! This is the perfect blend of flavors," one judge said with a mouthful of honey.

"Prepare yourselves, class. The next thing to happen changed the course of history forever." The class sat on the edge of their seats. "Kodiak and Gobi were so excited about their win, they hugged! This was the first documented bear hug in history!" The class cheered.

"After the honey standoff, Kodiak and Gobi opened a honey shop together, called *The Sweetest Victory*. Every customer left the shop with the best honey and the best bear hug. Unlike many other feuds in history, The Great Honey Feud of 1902 ended up being a sweet victory for everyone."

*Thank you to those who challenge me
and the world to be better everyday.
We need you.
H. S.*

The Sweetest Victory
Copyright © 2019 Hillary B. Spangler, MD

ALL RIGHTS RESERVED. This book contains material protected under International and Federal Copyright Laws and Treaties. Any unauthorized reprint or use of this material is prohibited.

No part of this book may be reproduced or transmitted in any form or by any means, electronic or mechanical, including photocopying, recording, or by any information storage and retrieval system without express written permission from the author.

Published by spanglernest
www.spanglernest.com

Printed in the United States of America

llustrated by Marina Saumell
www.marimell.com

ISBN: 978-0-9906-598-7-7